For my little sister, Ayoung

Farrar Straus Giroux Books for Young Readers
175 Fifth Avenue, New York 10010


Color separations by Bright Arts (H.K.) Ltd.
Printed in China by South China Printing Co. Ltd.,
Dongguan City, Guangdong Province
Designed by Roberta Pressel
First edition, 2014
1 3 5 7 9 10 8 6 4 2

mackids.com

Library of Congress Cataloging-in-Publication Data
Yum, Hyewon.
The twins' little sister / Hyewon Yum. — First edition.
pages cm
Summary: Twin sisters who already compete for their mother's attention have an especially hard time after their baby sister is born.
ISBN 978-0-374-37973-5 (hardcover)
[1. Twins—Fiction. 2. Sisters—Fiction. 3. Mother and child—Fiction. 4. Babies—Fiction.] I. Title.
PZ7.Y89656Tx 2014
[E]—dc23

2013013078

# the twins' little sister

hyewon yum

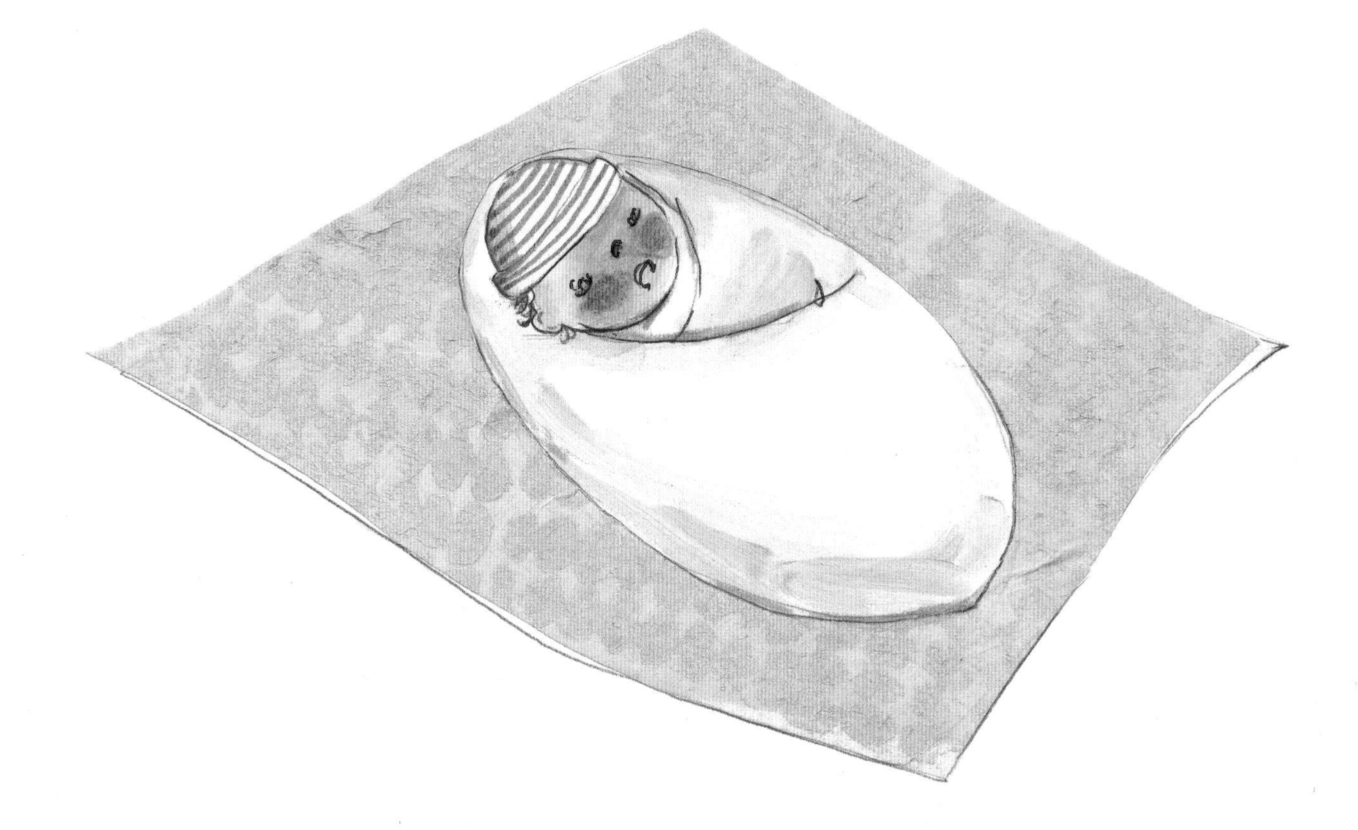

FRANCES FOSTER BOOKS
farrar straus giroux
new york

We're twin sisters, so we have two of everything.

We have two twin beds, two polka-dot dresses,
two baby dolls, two baby strollers . . .

but we have only one mom.

This is a big problem.

When we take a nap in the big grown-up bed,
I want Mom to look at me.

No, look at me. She's my mom!

And I want Mom to push me first when we're on the swings.

No, push me! Push me!

Mom says we can't fight over her anymore because we're going to have a little sister very soon.

And that means we're going to be big sisters.
This will be an even bigger problem.

Mom has only two arms.
Who's going to hold the baby's hand?

You're right!
Look, Mom can't run fast enough now,
and the baby's not even here yet.

Mom brings the baby home anyway
when we get back from Grandma's.

The baby is red and ugly.

She looks like the bread
in a paper bag.

Now Mom's grown-up bed doesn't have room for either of us.

We have to push each other on the swings while Mom stays with the baby on the bench.

Mom doesn't even have one hand for us.
I want my mom back.

But she's too busy to play.
What can we do?

Mom definitely needs my help.
I'll bring a clean diaper for the baby.

Mom says she's proud of me for being such a great big sister.

Well, I'm a great big sister, too!
I'll give the baby her pacifier.

Mom says it's not easy to make the baby stop crying.

But I can make her smile with the rattle!
I bet she thinks I'm the better big sister.

No way!
She laughs when I do peekaboo.
She likes me more!

She fell asleep when I sang to her.

Don't be silly!
She's asleep because I gave her my bunny.

Shh, you're too loud!
You'll wake her up!
She's kind of cute!
Isn't she?

She's adorable.

And she looks just like me.

I think it's okay to share our mom with her, don't you?

Yes, I'm so glad we have a baby sister.

The only problem now is we need another one.

I'll push the stroller!

No, it's my turn!